D0528877

Sitting
Ducks
TM

First published 2002 by Walker Books Ltd
87 Vauxhall Walk, London SE11 5HJ

2 4 6 8 10 9 7 5 3 1

© 2002 Universal Pictures Visual Programming Ltd
™Sitting Ducks Productions
Licensed by Universal Studios Licensing LLLP

Printed in Italy

All rights reserved

British Library Cataloguing in Publication Data:
a catalogue record for this book is available
from the British Library

ISBN 0-7445-9492-8

Born To Be Wild

Story by Michael Bedard and Richard Liebmann-Smith
Adapted by Charlie Gardner

"What'll it be, boys?" Bev waited impatiently on Ed, Oly and Waddle.

"Milkshakes!" they chorused.

"Uh-huh..." Bev raised an eyebrow suspiciously. "And who's going to pay?"

The three ducks pointed at each other. "Him!" they replied.

"That's what I figured!" Bev laughed. "OK, three waters coming up!"

She hurried back to the counter.

Distracted, Waddle looked out the window. What was that, gleaming gold on the pavement? Might it be a coin?

Coolly he hopped down from the table and wandered outside. It *was* a coin! Waddle smiled. "Oh boy! One milkshake, comin' up!"

Vroooooooooom! A shiny blue scooter roared up to the café. Waddle's eyes widened, and he almost forgot his new-found riches – this was the most beautiful two-wheeler he had ever seen...

PATO
EL PATO

"Nice wheels, huh, kid?" the rider said smugly. "Keep an eye on it, willya?" And, looking sharp in his leathers, he strutted into the Decoy.

"Keep an eye on it?" echoed Waddle, dreamily. He glanced over to the café – no one was watching him. Surely the owner wouldn't mind if he just kept the seat warm for a while...?

It wasn't long before Waddle was pretending to ride it full throttle: "Brrrrrrrm, brrrrm!" It was almost as good as the real thing.

Waddle struck a cool pose and flipped his coin – but missed the catch! Bending down to retrieve the money from the gutter, his wing brushed the starter switch; immediately the motor sprang into life and the bike zoomed away ... with Waddle hanging on for dear life!

"I may be wrong," said Oly, casually, "but I think I just saw Waddle on a scooter." And turning away from the window, he went back to sipping his water through a straw.

Waddle zoomed past again – he was having the ride of his life! At first he'd struggled to find his balance, but now he was just plain showing off.

"Hey – that *is* Waddle!" gasped Bill excitedly.

"And that's my scooter!" yelled the scooter duck.

Soon the entire café crowd was out on the pavement watching the show. Playing to his audience, Waddle turned the bike round for one last pass and roared down the street. Waddle looked good – Waddle looked cool – Waddle looked... SPLAT! A bug smacked into his face, his wings flailed and the bike wobbled out of control. The crowd dived for cover as the scooter careened by and – CRASH! – disappeared into the Decoy Café.

"He wrecked my scooter!" screamed the owner, furiously. But everyone else was much more interested in Waddle – his limp body lay sprawled across the floor of the Decoy.

"He's a dead duck," Bev pronounced solemnly.

"No, he's just out cold," Aldo reassured them.

Bill gave Waddle a shower with a glass of water. "Waddle! Waddle, are you OK?"

Waddle blinked his eyes and stared blankly around the café.

"Quack!" he exclaimed.

The customers looked puzzled. "'Quack'?"

"Quack, quack, quack!" Waddle continued, pecking at the leftovers on the floor. Everyone was amused until, tired of using the floor as a plate, Waddle decided to use it as a toilet instead!

"Ooooh, yuck!" groaned the Decoy diners. "How disgusting!"

"Calm down, everyone," said Bill. "Something's wrong with Waddle."

"Yeah," ranted the scooter duck. "He wrecked my scooter!"

Bev went into the kitchen and ladled something from a steaming cauldron. She placed a huge bowl of soup on the counter. "Cream of Pond Scum Soup!" she announced proudly. Waddle quacked quizzically. "Trust me," she continued. "A couple of sips of this and you'll be your old self in no time."

Waddle eyed up the bowl ... then jumped in and started swimming!

"This is serious," said Bill.

"It's worse than when he was just stupid," added Ed.

"I wonder what's the matter?" mused Aldo.

"This may sound strange," said Bill, thoughtfully, "but I think that bump on the head has turned him wild ... like us, before we were civilized."

"You mean – he's acting like a 'duck'?" said Bev.

"Exactly," Bill continued. "He's become a primitive!"

That evening, Waddle was out of the soup but paddling in Ed's bathtub instead.

Ed was at a loss. "This is pathetic. What are we going to do with him?"

"Maybe we could just leave him there," Oly replied. "It's not like we take baths."

"Good thinking," smiled Ed.

But the next morning, Ed and Oly wished they hadn't left Waddle on his own – the wild duck was nowhere to be found. They gazed into the empty bathtub while Bill and Aldo looked for clues.

"There's no way he could have gotten out of here," said Oly, puzzled.

"Hey – the window's open!" exclaimed Aldo. "Maybe he got out that way."

"But how?" asked Bill. "We're on the third floor!"

Ed peered out of the window – and gasped in horror! There was Waddle, atop a 100-foot-high billboard, quacking and flapping for all to see.

"B-but … but … that's impossible," Bill stammered. "How could he? Unless…"

Raoul flew in and perched on a telegraph pole. "Hey! Is he CRAY-zee? Howzee get up there?"

"Who knows?" Bill answered. "Maybe he ... FLEW?"

"Tha's ridiculous," Raoul snorted. "You city ducks don' fly. And he's so fat! Don' make me laugh..."

But Ed, Oly, Bill and Aldo had already rushed to the foot of the billboard and were struggling with a large ladder.

"Who's going to get him down?" Oly asked nervously.

"The strongest, of course," said Ed, looking at Aldo.

"Uh-uh. Alligators are afraid of heights." Aldo grimaced.

"It's Bill's ladder," Oly cut in.

"Yeah, it's Bill's ladder!" echoed Ed.

Suddenly all eyes were on Bill. "All right, all right. I'll go up and get him." And he started slowly up the ladder, feet flapping against the rungs...

"Don't look down, Bill!" said Aldo, unhelpfully.

Bill looked down. The ground below looked blurry, and he started to shake; the ladder was trembling alarmingly! He quickly looked back up and scrambled his way to the top as fast as he could.

"Waddle," coaxed Bill, "come to the ladder!"

"Quack!" Waddle replied – and walked *away* from the ladder.

Bill gulped. There was nothing for it … he would have to climb onto the billboard. Nervously he clambered up and wobbled his way along the edge like a clown on a tightrope. "I knew it … you *did* fly up here, didn't you!"

"Quack, quack!" replied Waddle, teetering on the edge of the billboard and stretching his wings.

As much as Bill wanted to see if Waddle really could fly, he dared not risk it. Forgetting his fear of heights for a moment, he ran to Waddle and tried to grab him; but the pair of them toppled off the edge and into oblivion…

"AAAAAAAAAAGH!" Bill and Waddle plummeted through the air towards the ground. Ed, Oly and Aldo looked on in horror.

Out of the blue, Raoul appeared. Adjusting his wings for a power dive he tracked the two ducks and started cracking jokes. "Oh … so we are flying now, huh?"

"No, we're FALLING!" Bill shrieked, as calmly as he could.

Raoul let out a shrill whistle and two more crows flew in from nowhere like a pair of feathery fighter jets. They swooped down, flew low and effortlessly scooped up Bill and Waddle just seconds before impact. Then, as if by magic, they slowly and gently floated to a safe touchdown on the ground.

"Well!" said Raoul, preening himself. "Now I think we know who should be flyin' in the sky, and who should be ridin' on the bus!"

Waddle was back to his old self, and the news had got round Ducktown faster than free milkshakes in the Decoy. Bill and Waddle were mobbed in the street.

Oly rushed forward to embrace his friend. "He's back!"

"He's Waddle!" confirmed Ed.

"He's hungry!" was all Waddle could say.

That evening, Bill sat on his balcony contemplating all that had happened. How could Waddle have got to the top of a billboard? Was it really possible that he had flown? Perhaps they would never know...

Bill sighed and folded a piece of paper into a dart. He launched the aeroplane and watched it spiral over the rooftops and into the sunset. Might a duck fly?

One day, maybe... One day...